For Huw and William

Clarion Books
a Houghton Mifflin Company imprint
215 Park Avenue South, New York, NY 10003
Copyright © 2001 by John Richardson

Fist published in Great Britain in 2001 by Hutchinson Children's Books,
The Random House Group Limited, 20 Vauxhall Bridge Road, London SW1V 2SA.

The illustrations were executed in watercolor.
The text was set in 18-point Columbus.

www.houghtonmifflinbooks.com

Printed in Singapore.

Library of Congress Cataloging-in-Publication Data

Richardson, John, 1955–
Grunt / John Richardson.
p. cm.
Summary: Teased by his older siblings about his appearance and tiny squeal, a little piggy finds acceptance with
an equally odd-looking companion who teaches him to celebrate his differences and recognize
that others will appreciate his uniqueness, too.
ISBN 0-618-15974-6
[1. Pigs—Fiction. 2. Self-acceptance—Fiction. 3. Individuality—Fiction.] I. Title.
PZ7.R39487 Gr 2001
[E]—dc21   2001037104

10 9 8 7 6 5 4 3 2 1

GRUNT

John Richardson

CLARION BOOKS

NEW YORK

A whiskery pig and his fine fat wife had six piglets.
The last and the least they called Wee-skin-and-bones.
   This little piggy had crinkly-crumply ears, a tiddly-
widdly button of a snout, and absolutely no tail at all.
And when he tried to squeal, all that came out was a
teeny-tiny grunt.

His brothers and sisters, however, were big, beautiful, plump piggies with flippy-flappy ears, big snuffly-snorty snouts, and curly-whirly tails. But they were unkind to their tiny brother.

"He's not playing with *us!*" they squealed.

"He's got no tail to wiggle and squiggle."

"His snout is too small to snuffle and truffle."

"His ears don't go flippety-flappety."

"He's just a Wee-skin-and-bones."

The whiskery papa pig didn't seem to notice him at all. But what made Wee-skin-and-bones especially sad was that his brothers and sisters made so much noise his mama couldn't hear his tiny grunts.

"Nobody loves me," sobbed Wee-skin-and-bones.

"Cock-a-doodle-doo! What'll little piggy do?" crowed the rooster.

"Me-oh-my! He can't stay in the sty," bleated the sheep.

"Neigh-neigh-neigh! You must go away!" cried the horse.

"Off you go, then," said the fat speckled hen.

So Wee-skin-and-bones ran wee-wee-wee all the way from home until he reached the middle of a great dark forest.

High above him, the cold moon shone in the black night sky.

He thought about his warm bed of straw. He thought about his brothers and sisters. He thought about his mama and papa.

And he cried a whole puddle of tears.

An owl hooted. Leaves rustled.
Wee-skin-and-bones rubbed his
eyes and looked hard into the shadows.
Two beady eyes looked back at him.
"What's the matter, little piggy?" asked a
wonderfully kind voice.
"I'm Wee-skin-and-bones, and I'm all alone in the
big wide world."
"Then it's good that I'm here," said the voice. "My name
is Old-scratch-and-scruff. I'm a bristly old scruff on the outside,
but inside…Oooo…I'm a *beauty!* Will you be my friend?"

"Me! How can I be your friend," sighed Wee-skin-and-bones, "when I have no tail to wiggle and squiggle?"

"Tails?" said Old-scratch-and-scruff. "I can take 'em or leave 'em."

"But my ears are all crinkly and crumply, I've got a tiddly-widdly snout, and no one can hear my teeny-tiny grunt."

"Crinkly! Crumply! Tiddly! Widdly!" cried Old-scratch-and-scruff. "Wonderful! Couldn't be better! And I can hear you just fine."

Old-scratch-and-scruff led the little piggy to the warmth and safety of his den. He gave him supper and then tucked him into a bed of moss and leaves.

"Good night, Wee-skin-and-bones," whispered the scruffy boar.

In the morning, Old-scratch-and-scruff took
Wee-skin-and-bones for a romp through
the forest. They jumped in puddles. They
chased leaves on the breeze.

They snuffled for truffles.

They pulled
plums off the trees.

Suddenly, Wee-skin-and-bones let out such a big grunt that he startled Old-scratch-and-scruff. "What's this feeling I've got?" he gasped. "Like…"

"Like you've a tail that's curly and whirly?" said
Old-scratch-and-scruff.

"And like my ears are flippy-flappy. And my snout is
all snuffly and snorty," finished Wee-skin-and-bones.

"That's *happy!*" cried Old-scratch-and-scruff. "Happy inside out!"

"But…" said the little piggy.

"There's something missing?" finished the boar.

"Yes," said Wee-skin-and-bones.

All of a sudden, there was a great snorting and snuffling and squeaking and squealing. Wee-skin-and-bones's mama came trundling up the hill, with her babies following close behind.

She took one look at Wee-skin-and-bones and burst into a
whole torrent of tears.

"There you are!" she cried. "I've been searching
everywhere for you."

"Oh," said Wee-skin-and-bones, "you don't mind
that I'm all tiddly-widdly and crinkly-crumply?"

"Crinkly-crumply, tiddly-widdly…is even *more* precious," said the fine mama pig, smothering her baby in a whole shower of kisses.

"GRUNT!" grunted Wee-skin-and-bones very loudly and happily.

"My thoughts exactly!" said Old-scratch-and-scruff,
as he quietly slipped back into the forest.